Phoebe-Bear
If You DARE

A tale of an Irish Wolfhound puppy with personality
and her adventures with her crazy family.

Celene Anne Collison
Art by Jupiters Muse

Tellwell Talent
www.tellwell.ca

ISBN
978-0-2288-5718-1 (Hardcover)
978-0-2288-5717-4 (Paperback)

Acknowledgements

To my family, Kris, Karson and Oskar, for indulging my great love of the Irish Wolfhound. Much love to Christy Hagen and Grandma Sandy for their endless encouragement. Thanks to Lona Collison for creative feedback about character and colour.

To great neighbours, the Dixons, for the long walks with Matilda, a Great Dane. Thanks to Ralph and Lori Gerbig for many fun evening walks with Willow, a Border Terrier.

To amazing people, like Emma Ross, who are completely dedicated to the breed's health. A giant thanks to Alexis Scoutari for welcoming Phoebe into her home while we were on vacation.

To Dustin and Jordan Dawick for always saying yes to pet sitting Phoebe and Phisher. We are so grateful to you both. To Jelena Cote-Gaudet Tumin for always believing in me!

To Chamyli Denis, Andrew, Adelaine, and Jordan Geil for their extra sets of eyes. I'm very grateful to Laura Hulme for her friendship and scrutinizing eye for commas. What would I do without friends who are avid readers?

To my editor, Ann Marie, for her positivity and great feedback through all three rounds of editing. Thanks to Grace Gange, my project manager, for keeping me on track. Thanks to Jupiters Muse for bringing my vision to life through all the revisions.

To the Irish Wolfhound community for sharing decades of knowledge about the breed. It's been a giant ride to have my first hound, Phoebe Scarlet Collison Kretz.

Preface

Phoebe-Bear brings smiles to faces big and small. She is mighty and so very tall. We've met many neighbours because of her. A Wolfhound is really quite the lure.

Kids are often in awe of her sweet giant face. She makes you slow down from life's frantic pace. "Take your sniffs" is her motto. It's not a race.

Phoebe-Bear makes you stare. She is a majestic Wolfhound if you dare. She is a beautiful beast, a treasure, and a special soul, to say the least.

A wolf hunter, nonetheless, she is gentle when stroked but, fierce when provoked. Her eyes are always gazing at the horizon. If something moves, the chase is on. After all, that is Wolfhound fun!

Once upon a time, my humans lived in a charming Canadian city. They called it New Westminster, and it sure was pretty. They wanted a giant dog so very, very badly! They searched far and wide but, had no luck sadly. At last, they found me, a Wolfhound pup, to be by their side.

4

On the way home, I was still a little nervous, you see. I sat on my new brother Oskar and had a little pee. He looked at me with shock and surprise. "Don't you dare stare at me," I thought! "I may be cute and small now, but one day I'll be giant and tall."

6

We arrived home to a great big house. There stood this furry thing they called a cat. Phisher was his name, and he was even hairier than a rat! So, there I sat, staring at this thing, a so called "cat." I tried to chase it, but they said, "Phoebe-Bear, no chasing that!"

7

At first, I was a bit like a shark biting everything in sight. Mom said, "Phoebe-Bear, you are quite a fright!" I even bit my brother's arm, but really, I meant no harm. I couldn't help it, you see. My teeth hurt bad, so I needed something to chew. A basketball, I decided would do.

I loved my little brother Oskar so much! He gave me lots of kisses and had the perfect touch. Whenever he put his shoes on, I knew he was leaving for school. I was no fool. He'd say, "Phoebe-Bear, be good and don't steal any food."

And then one fall day, I discovered this green stuff called clover. Mom said, "Phoebe-Bear, please don't roll in it over and over and over!" You see, every time I got near it, I got a little silly. Mom said, "It must be the Irish in me." I only stopped when I got too chilly.

10

Mom took me for coffee after a big play at the park. The barista gave me a cup full of this yummy white stuff. From then on, whenever I saw a coffee cup, I began to bark. Mom said, "Phoebe-Bear, you silly pup. You can't have a 'puppacino' at every coffee stop."

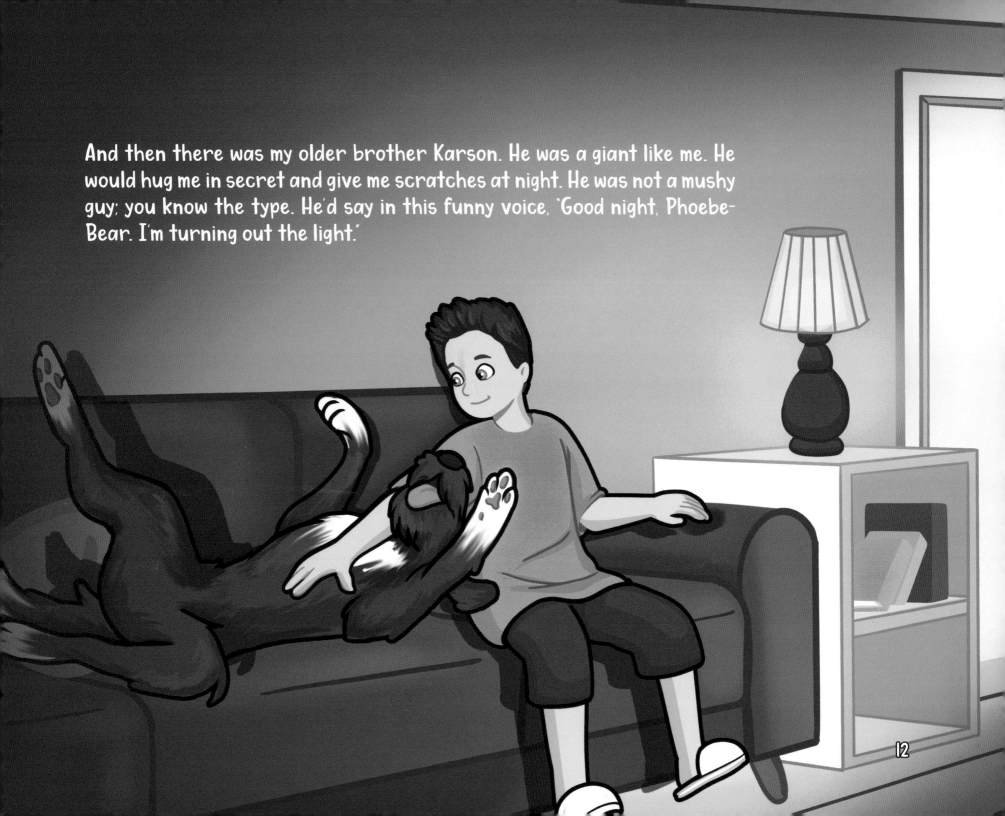

And then there was my older brother Karson. He was a giant like me. He would hug me in secret and give me scratches at night. He was not a mushy guy; you know the type. He'd say in this funny voice, 'Good night, Phoebe-Bear. I'm turning out the light.'

Mom got a ramp and would say, "Hurry up" or "HUP" for short. I would stare at her hard till she'd say, "Phoebe-Bear, what's up?" Then I would stroll up the ramp but just to get a treat. It was the only way to get me moving, and to mom, it was quite a feat. Some might call me stubborn, but I think of it as strong-willed. I'm an Irish princess after all.

13

Winter arrived and Mom decided I needed manners. We were off to puppy class to learn the training basics fast. I could even do a puppy push-up and was having a blast. The trainer said, "Phoebe-Bear, sit, down and up again." I was tired by then and fell into a downward dog.

14

I saw my first snowfall, and boy, it was great! This fluffy white stuff fell till it was quite late. I could stick my tongue out as far as my nose. I even caught snowballs in my mouth. Where they went, nobody knows. Mom said, "Phoebe-Bear, what do you think?" I was hooked, and then my paws started to sink, sink, sink.

Mom put strange boots on me to protect my giant paws. She said, "Phoebe-Bear, you need them to keep warm and cozy." I got up awkwardly, and my cheeks were kind of rosy. Then I started to hop around like a dizzy bunny. If only you could have seen it. Boy, it was certainly funny!

16

I had my first Christmas and, oh, what a joy! I thought Saint Nick might bring me a toy. The humans put up a great big tree. The boys opened my stocking with absolute glee. Oskar said, "Phoebe-Bear, let me see!" But after all the hustle and bustle, I was tired and needed a deep sleep.

ZZZ.

I picked up a funny habit that brought me lots of giggles. While Mom tried to clean, I'd steal her paper towel roll for fun. She'd chase me around the house as fast as my legs would wiggle. "Phoebe-Bear, drop it!" Mom would say in a high-pitched voice. "No, I would not, thanks a lot!" I thought.

One day, Mom met a neighbour named Dustin and they started to talk. He screeched in delight when he saw us on a walk. To my surprise, he had a "wolfie," named "Ava," like me. She was blonde and sweet as the honey from a bee. We later met at the park and had a cup of tea under a tree.

19

After a long winter, my family wanted a "vacay." I thought it best to do a homestay. My dog walker, Pascale, moved into the house. She was French Canadian and cute as a mouse. But I missed my family and was very, very mad. So, I ate the sofa, and Mom said, "Phoebe-Bear, you are very, very bad!"

Pascale took me on hikes with many other dogs. I was part of her pack until my family got back. It was cool until I came down with a cough. Mom was so sad to see me feeling so rough. She said, "Phoebe-Bear, I really do care!" Thank goodness she came home because I needed her there.

21

Spring arrived and the sun came out. The flowers popped up, and I sniffed them with my very long snout. Mom put her arms around me as close as could be. She said, "I love you, Phoebe-Bear," and then she kissed me.

22

We had a special bond, Mom and me. It was not one that the plain eye could see. We did everything together, and she always talked to me. Phoebe-Bear was the nickname she called me. I looked into her eyes with such a soulful stare. I captured her heart right from the start.

23

Before I knew it, a year was done, and I was now turning one. Mom said, "It's your birthday! Let's put on a hat and have some fun!" I looked at her in horror. She said, "Phoebe-Bear, turn that frown upside down."

"This is inhumane," I thought, "or maybe Mom has gone insane?"

24

Summer was here once again.
Mom said, "Phoebe-Bear, dear, let's visit your dog family!"

"Oh boy, oh boy, oh boy!" I thought, jumping with joy. You see, I hadn't seen my dog parents in almost a year. My dog mother's name was Eba, and we looked a lot alike. My dog father was Riley. He was as big as a bike!

25

After our visit, we packed up our stuff and loaded me into the car. Mom said, "Come on, you sweet pup, we are driving very, very far. Finally, we arrived at the wild West Coast and what a beautiful sight! The beach was long, and the sand was so soft, much to my delight. "Phoebe-Bear, we made it. Now, let's have a marshmallow roast."

A week had gone by, and we had to drive home. I was stuck in the car again! I wanted to go back to the beach, there was no doubt. Mom said, "Phoebe-Bear, please don't pout. I know, it's a shame you can't live in paradise forever, you beautiful dame."

27

It was the middle of summer, and the house was hot, hot, hot! Mom said, "Phoebe-Bear, we must walk early; otherwise, we shall not." You see, I didn't like the heat. I didn't like it at all. It made my tongue hang out right down to my feet.

28

Fall was approaching, and Mom started to notice I was growing like a weed. She said, "Phoebe-Bear, whatever is the matter? Tell me what you need?" It was a little embarrassing, but I couldn't fit in her car. What I needed was a school bus so there would be room for me without the fuss.

29

Then our lovely neighbours asked if I wanted to meet their Great Dane. Indeed, she was a giant, and Matilda was her name. So, we arranged to meet at a local dog park. We had so much fun, and before we knew it, we were playing a wrestling game. Best friends forever and ever, we soon became.

Before I knew it, a year had flown by since I had met my humans. They called it "Gotcha Day." Mom said it was special and it was time to sing. "Phoebe-Bear, we love you so much and can't believe it's been a year! We are so glad you're part of this family, my sweet, sweet dear."

Phoebe-Bear is my nickname, you see. My family loves me like crazy. I am an Irish Wolfhound, if you care, and I have the heart of a teddy bear. My family thinks I'm so much fun. I always have them on the run. Stay tuned for more adventures with me if you dare ... XO Phoebe-Bear.

32

About the Author

Celene Collison is excited to be the author of her first children's book about an Irish Wolfhound puppy growing up with an urban family. It's based on the true story of Celene's hilarious experience of owning a giant dog.

Celene is an animal advocate and a huge dog lover. She believes animals connect humans and bring a lot of joy to the world. Celene has a marketing background and has been a stay-at-home mom for the past ten years.

After deciding to get such a giant dog, the book evolved as a natural passion project. Celene lives in New Westminster, British Columbia, Canada, with her human and furry family. The crazy household includes her fiancé (Kris), two boys (Karson and Oskar), Phisher (the cat), and of course Princess Phoebe-Bear (the Wolfhound).